THAT NAUGHTY MEERKAT!

For Liam Turcot-Jones, with love from his great-uncle across the water — I.W.

For Kyle and Codie — G.P.

First published in paperback in Great Britain by HarperCollins Children's Books in 2015
This edition published in 2016

10 9 8 7 6 5 4 3 2 1

ISBN: 978-0-00-813945-2

HarperCollins Children's Books is a division of HarperCollins Publishers Ltd.

Text copyright © Ian Whybrow 2015, 2016
Illustrations copyright © Garry Parsons 2015

Visit our website at: www.harpercollins.co.uk

Printed in China

THAT NAUGHTY MEERKAT!

IAN WHYBROW Illustrated by GARRY PARSONS

HarperCollins *Children's Books*

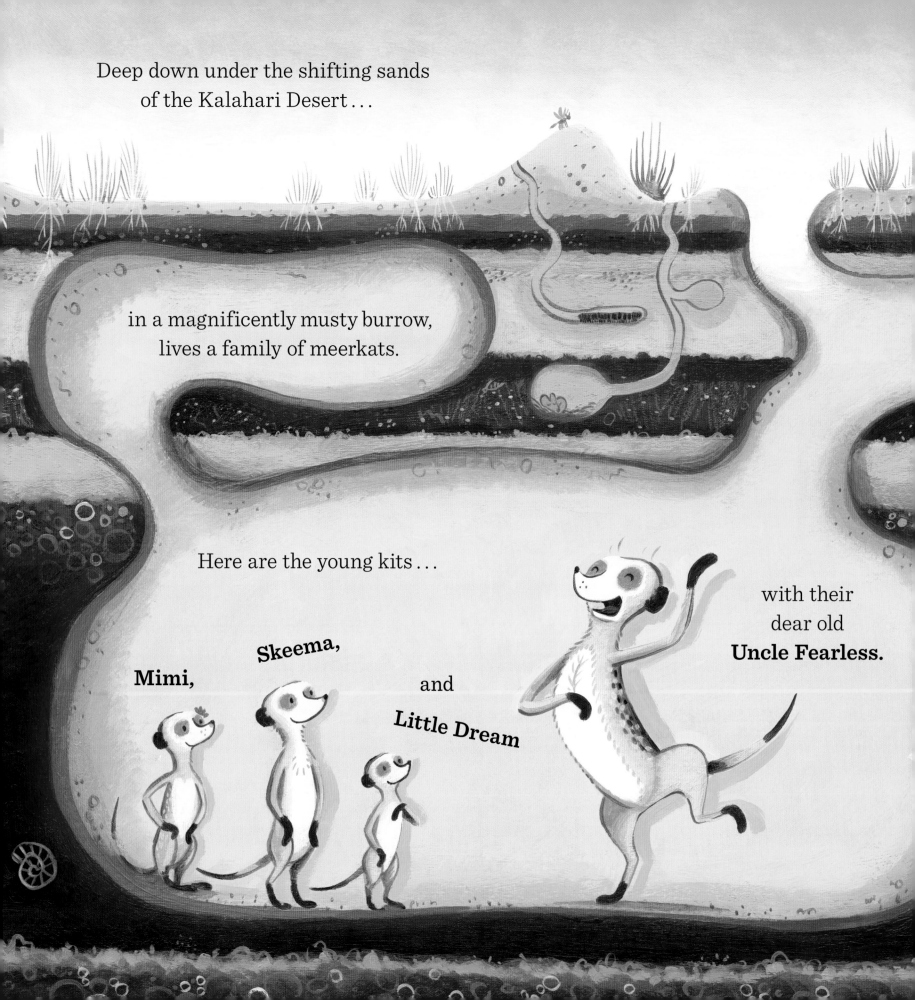

Deep down under the shifting sands
of the Kalahari Desert...

in a magnificently musty burrow,
lives a family of meerkats.

Here are the young kits...

Mimi,

Skeema,

and

Little Dream

with their
dear old
Uncle Fearless.

And here in the nursery, is **Radiant** with her four squeaky-squirmy new babies...

Bundle,

Zora,

Quickpaws

and that naughty meerkat, **TROUBLE.**

One morning, Radiant was feeling *exhausted*.

"Take the day off, my dear!" said Uncle Fearless. "I'll look after the babies."

"Are you sure?" said Radiant. "They can get into mischief, you know. Especially *Trouble*."

"*Nonsense!*"
said Uncle Fearless.

"I am a **proud chief**, remember!
I am **stern** and **wise**!

I have won fights with **snakes**
and **wild painted-dogs**!

No baby would dare to be a
bother with *me* in charge!"

So off went Radiant to have a happy day digging for scorpions, while the kits were off exploring.

"Follow me, babies!" ordered Uncle Fearless. "Quick march! Today I shall teach you the proper Meerkat Way of doing things!"

Up, up the tunnel and out into the warm sunshine went Zora, Bundle, Quickpaws, and finally...

Trouble.

"*Pay attention now!*" called Uncle Fearless
in his sternest voice. "It is still chilly out here.
So first, I shall teach you how we meerkats do
our morning warm-up. We point our belly buttons
toward the sun like this and go . . .

1-2-3 Hup!"

All the **good** babies copied him, with a ...

1-2-3

Hup!

But guess which naughty baby pointed his *bottom* at the sun?

Yes ...

Trouble!

So, then Zora started *dancing around*…

and Bundle tried to *stand on his head*…

and Quickpaws *had a scratch*…

so now none of them were doing what Uncle Fearless said!

"Babies, behave!"
shouted Uncle Fearless.

"Especially you, Trouble!"

Just then, Mimi, Little Dream,
and Skeema popped up.

"It looks like you could do with
some help, Uncle Fearless,"
offered Mimi.

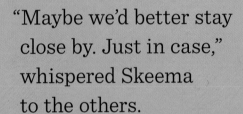

"Nonsense!"
said Uncle Fearless.

"I am a **proud chief**,
remember! I am **stern**
and **wise**!

I have won fights with **snakes**
and **wild painted-dogs!**

No baby would dare to be a
bother with *me* in charge!"

"Maybe we'd better stay
close by. Just in case,"
whispered Skeema
to the others.

Next, it was time to learn digging —
the Meerkat Way.

"Watch carefully this time, babies!"
Uncle Fearless ordered. "We open
our back legs like this and shoot
the sand through!"

All the babies did perfect digging, except for . . .

that naughty meerkat, **Trouble!**
He shot the sand all over the others!
Zora started to cough . . .
and Bundle started to squeak . . .

and Quickpaws got covered completely.

"Babies, behave!"
shouted Uncle Fearless.
"*TROUBLE!* That is not
the Meerkat Way to do digging!"

"Uncle Fearless, are you *sure*
you don't need any help?"
called Little Dream from
behind a tree.

"Me? Need help!"
spluttered Uncle Fearless.

"I am a **proud chief**, remember!
I am **stern** and **wise**!

I have won fights with **snakes**
and **wild painted-dogs**!

No baby would dare to be a
bother with *me* in charge!"

But Mimi could see that Uncle Fearless was quite worn out. "You know, Uncle," she said, "what babies really like doing is playing. Come and see."

And she led everyone
to the top of a nearby
sand dune . . .

to the **Meerkat Adventure Playground!**

Soon the babies had learned:

how to slide down the ant heap,

how to dance
like a scorpion,

and how to roll stones
like a dung beetle!

While the young kits did the teaching, Uncle Fearless kept guard, just in case any snakes or wild painted-dogs should dare to come along.

Suddenly he spied a hungry eagle owl in the sky.

"Dive! Dive! Dive!"
ordered Uncle Fearless.

Quick as a tick, the meerkats
hurried into a nearby bolt hole.

But, oh no! Trouble got left behind!

Just in time,
Uncle Fearless grabbed Trouble
and bundled him down a bolt hole.

The eagle owl missed them
by a *whisker!*

When the day was over, Uncle Fearless cried,
"Well done, kits!"

"And well done, you, Uncle," said Mimi.
"You were ever so brave."

"Teamwork!" said Uncle Fearless.
"That's the Meerkat Way to do things."

That evening,
when Radiant came home,
the babies were having a quiet nap.

"How ever did you manage
to settle them all down?" she asked.
"Even Trouble!"

Uncle Fearless began to boast,
"I am a **proud chief,**
who is **stern** and **wise . . .** "

But then he said,
"Actually . . . no! I *couldn't* have done it by myself.
Thank goodness Skeema, Mimi, and Little Dream
were there to help me keep an eye out for . . .
Trouble."